the BAD GUYS

in

SUPERBAD

TEXT AND ILLUSTRATIONS COPYRIGHT © 2018 BY AARON BLABEY

ALL RIGHTS RESERVED. PUBLISHED BY SCHOLASTIC PRESS, AN IMPRINT OF SCHOLASTIC
INC., PUBLISHERS SINCE 1920. scholastic AND ASSOCIATED LOGOS ARE TRADEMARKS AND/
OR REGISTERED TRADEMARKS OF SCHOLASTIC INC. THIS EDITION PUBLISHED UNDER LICENSE
FROM SCHOLASTIC AUSTRALIA PTY LIMITED. FIRST PUBLISHED BY SCHOLASTIC AUSTRALIA PTY
LIMITED IN 2018.

THE PUBLISHER DOES NOT HAVE ANY CONTROL OVER AND DOES NOT ASSUME ANY
RESPONSIBILITY FOR AUTHOR OR THIRD-PARTY WEBSITES OR THEIR CONTENT.

NO PART OF THIS PUBLICATION MAY BE REPRODUCED, STORED IN A RETRIEVAL SYSTEM,
OR TRANSMITTED IN ANY FORM OR BY ANY MEANS, ELECTRONIC, MECHANICAL,
PHOTOCOPYING, RECORDING, OR OTHERWISE, WITHOUT WRITTEN PERMISSION OF THE PUBLISHER.
FOR INFORMATION REGARDING PERMISSION, WRITE TO SCHOLASTIC AUSTRALIA,
AN IMPRINT OF SCHOLASTIC AUSTRALIA PTY LIMITED, 345 PACIFIC HIGHWAY,
LINDFIELD NSW 2070 AUSTRALIA.

THIS BOOK IS A WORK OF FICTION. NAMES, CHARACTERS, PLACES, AND INCIDENTS ARE
EITHER THE PRODUCT OF THE AUTHOR'S IMAGINATION OR ARE USED FICTITIOUSLY, AND ANY
RESEMBLANCE TO ACTUAL PERSONS, LIVING OR DEAD, BUSINESS ESTABLISHMENTS,
EVENTS, OR LOCALES IS ENTIRELY COINCIDENTAL.

ISBN 978-1-338-18963-6

10 9 8 7 6 5 4 3 2 1   19 20 21 22 23

PRINTED IN THE U.S.A.   23
FIRST U.S. PRINTING 2019

· AARON BLABEY ·

the BAD GUYS

in

SUPERBAD

SCHOLASTIC INC.

Well, if he *does* know, honey,
he doesn't seem to care . . .

· CHAPTER 1 ·
IDIOTS ASSEMBLE

It's the
GOOD GUYS CLUB!

Ah yes!
But we are developing a
better name that will sound
much cooler, *señorita* . . .

Get on with it, man . . .

Yes! Of course!
You've messed with the wrong
planet, *hermanos.*

SUPER SPEED . . .

Oh man.
He did it again.
He, like, ran straight
into that thing . . .

Yeah, well, aliens?
I bet you weren't counting on . . .

THIS!

FOOOOOOF!

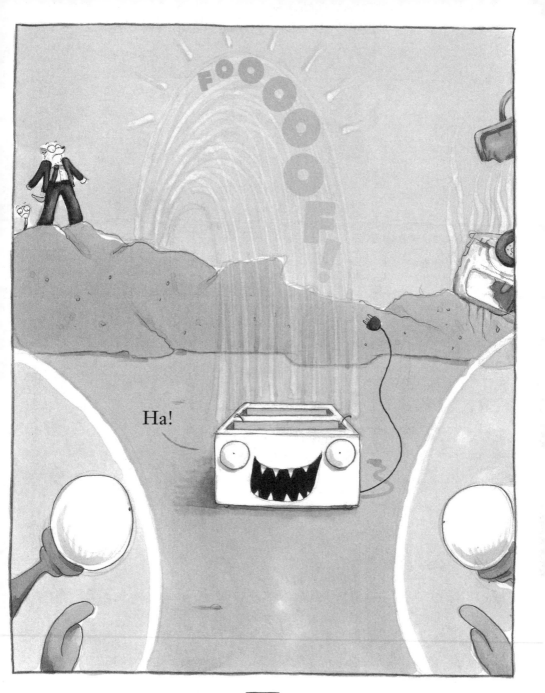

KER-CHINK!

Oh, no, no . . .
wait a minute . . .
hold that thought . . .

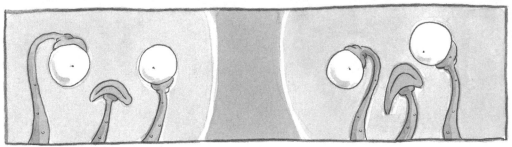

Aw, this is just embarrassing . . .

NO! These antics
have all been a
cunning trick to
distract you from
THIS!

Mr. Wolf!
WHAT ARE YOU DOING?!

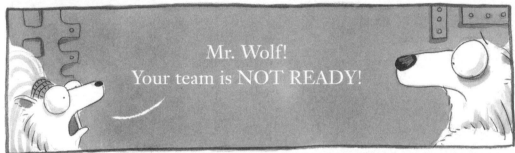

Mr. Wolf!
Your team is NOT READY!

What makes you say that?

I know your hearts are in the right place, but you need our help.

When we're finished with you, you'll be ready to take on **ANYTHING.**

Good Guys Club? Meet . . .

• CHAPTER 2 •
THE
LEAGUE

AGENT FOX

NAME: CLASSIFIED

PERSONAL HISTORY: CLASSIFIED

MASTER of SPYCRAFT

MASTER of MARTIAL ARTS

FLUENT in 14 LANGUAGES

PREFERRED VEHICLE: ANY

AGENT KITTY KAT

NAME: CLASSIFIED

PERSONAL HISTORY: CLASSIFIED

MASTER of MARTIAL ARTS

DOCTOR of MEDICINE

PILOT: FIRST CLASS

PREFERRED VEHICLE: AIRCRAFT

AGENT HOGWILD

NAME: CLASSIFIED

PERSONAL HISTORY: CLASSIFIED

DEMOLITIONS EXPERT

COMBAT SPECIALIST

PREFERRED VEHICLE: MOTORCYCLE

AGENT DOOM

NAME: CLASSIFIED

PERSONAL HISTORY: CLASSIFIED

COMPUTER HACKING GENIUS

DOCTOR of BIOLOGY, CHEMISTRY, PHYSICS, BIO-ENGINEERING + PHILOSOPHY

Meh.

AGENT SHORTFUSE

NAME:CLASSIFIED

PERSONAL HISTORY:CLASSIFIED

SPECIAL SKILLS:CLASSIFIED

CHAPTER 3

WHAT'S GOING ON

Welcome to our
SECRET HEADQUARTERS.
Now that you know a little bit about us,
let's talk about **YOU.**

Mr. Wolf, Mr. Snake, Mr. Shark, and Mr. Piranha—
the International League of Heroes is
well aware of your recent work, and
we've all been briefed on your . . .

NEW TALENTS.

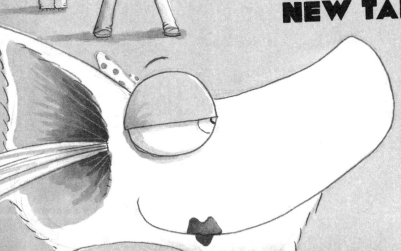

I'd also like to introduce my team to another very special member of the Good Guys Club—

LEGS!

Legs?
Are you OK?
You don't seem
your usual
cheerful self.

Huh?
Yeah.
I'm fine.
Just FINE.

He likes to be called Mr. Tarantula!

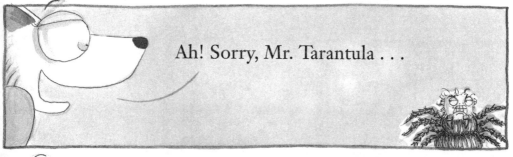

Ah! Sorry, Mr. Tarantula . . .

Yeah, yeah, *WHATEVER!*

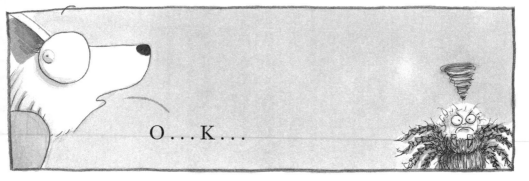

O . . . K . . .

It's the weirdest thing . . .
I just got you a muffin.

Aw, thanks!

And finally, the . . . er . . . newest
member of the Good Guys Club—
MILTON.

And yes, in case you're wondering,
Milton *does* appear to be a **DINOSAUR**
from the Cretaceous period . . .

A dinosaur with an IQ of **512.**
According to my tests, he's easily the **MOST INTELLIGENT BEING ON THE FACE OF THE EARTH.**

Does anyone want to explain that?

It's kind of creeping me out . . .

Oh, you're making me blush, dear lady—*really*!

What's a few hundred IQ points between friends? I'm just thrilled to be involved, and I must say, you all seem *lovely*.

Who'd care for a cup of tea?

Yep, that just happened.

Seriously, am I the only one creeped out by him?

Sooooo, obviously something highly unusual happened to all of you when you passed through that **VORTEX.**

Milton became **HYPER-INTELLIGENT . . .**

I really like her. She's *delightful*, don't you think?

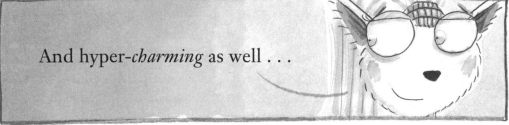

And hyper-*charming* as well . . .

On the other hand,
Mr. Piranha has

SUPER SPEED.

Mr. Shark can

SHAPE-SHIFT.

Mr. Snake has rather remarkable

MIND POWERS . . .

Well, they're not THAT remarkable . . .

Now you're going to *GET ME A TRUMPET.*

Now I'm going to GET YOU A TRUMPET . . .

Yeah, they're pretty remarkable. But you're kind of **MEAN**, aren't you?

Trumpet . . .

Oh wow.
So many sore spots . . .

POKE!
POKE!
POKE!

Yeah, yeah.
Run away, "Mr. Remarkable."
I've got my eye on you.

And as for
MR. WOLF . . .

Aw, he's just a good old-fashioned **NUDIST!**
You looked FINE out there today,
baaaybeeee . . .

Play nice, Agent Hogwild.

As we all know, Mr. Wolf has
SUPER STRENGTH.

Unfortunately, though, there's a **PROBLEM.**
Other than Milton, none of you are able to fully **CONTROL** your powers . . .

I'VE GOT POWERS!
I DO! AND I *CAN CONTROL THEM!*
LOOK! I'VE GOT **CRAZY SPIDER POWERS...**

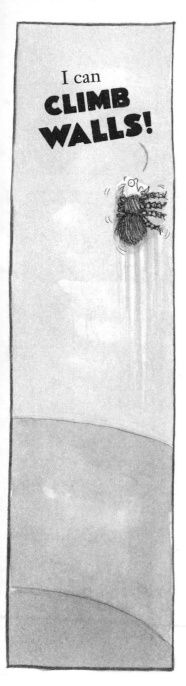

I can **CLIMB WALLS!**

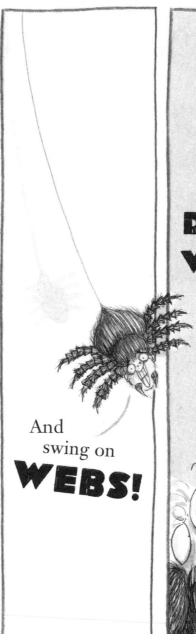

And swing on **WEBS!**

And I have **DEADLY VENOM!!**

Ahhh . . . I think that's just called **BEING A SPIDER** isn't it?

Yeah, buddy. It kind of is.

But that's why we LOVE YOU, *chico*! You're just the **SAME OLD MR. TARANTULA!**

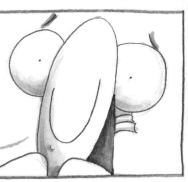

WHY DIDN'T I GET SUPERPOWERS?!

Ohhh, THAT'S why you're grouchy . . .

I'M NOT GROUCHY!

Dear boy, it pains me to see you like this.

If I *had* to hazard a guess as to why you weren't transformed like the rest of us, I'd suggest it *might* be because you passed through the vortex **BEFORE** your Bolivian friend switched on the **ENHANCEMENT DRIVE...**

HOW *DARE* YOU!
I didn't switch on ANYTHING!

Are you certain?
It was probably marked
DO NOT PRESS or
something like that . . .

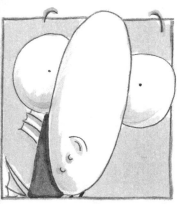

Look!
A cloud shaped
like a peanut . . .

You like peanuts?
Why don't we go out tonight and
get a whole crate of peanuts?

That sounds like **FUN.**
I bet you're a
good dancer, too.
Wanna go dancin'?

It doesn't really matter **HOW** you were transformed. What matters is this: You have powers that—if **PROPERLY HARNESSED**— could help defeat the terrible

ALIEN FORCES

spreading across the planet.

I cannot lie, the situation is not looking good . . .

Their **MOTHER SHIPS** have settled above every major city.

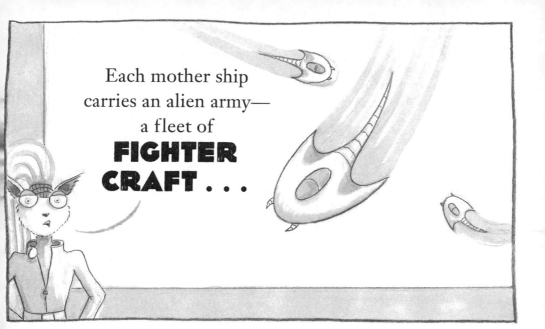

Each mother ship carries an alien army— a fleet of **FIGHTER CRAFT . . .**

and a legion of **ROBOT WAR MACHINES** used by the aliens on the ground.

The aliens are able to

CHANGE THEIR SIZE AT WILL.

They can be gigantic one minute and then shrink down to

fit inside the helmet of a **WAR MACHINE.**

That's how **MARMALADE**

disguised himself as a guinea pig.

They are HIGHLY ADVANCED.

They are HOSTILE.

And they are **EVERYWHERE.**

Well in that case, I'd better put my **ENORMOUS BRAIN** to work and come up with a **PLAN.**

BUT!
I'll need an assistant!
And there's only one name
at the top of my list—
MR. TARANTULA,
I need you!
I suspect you're more
important to our survival
than you think . . .

Yeah, OK,
*what*ever.

Goodness!
I've just realized
you are entirely
without pants!

Yeah, well, get over it.

And as for the rest of you . . .

It's **TRAINING DAY.**

· CHAPTER 4 ·
BE A TEACUP

Lesson One—
DON'T ANNOY ME.

Lesson Two?

Be a teacup.

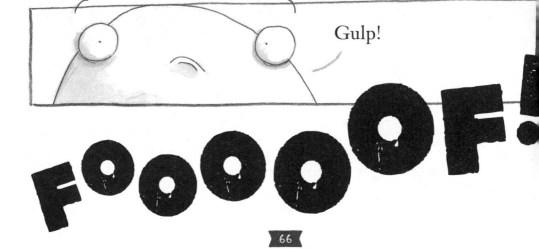

Gulp!

FOOOOOOF!

72

But can you be a teacup . . .

when it matters?

SSSSSSSSSSS!

· CHAPTER 5 ·
TURN! TURN! TURN!

What's going on here?!
Why are we in this

TINY METAL ROOM?

Well . . . we're
going to play
a **GAME.**

Oh . . . OK . . . I like games.
What kind of game?

It's my favorite.

 Really? What's it called?

 HOGWILD CHASE

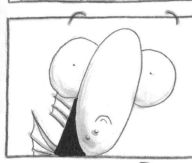

 What does that involve . . . ?

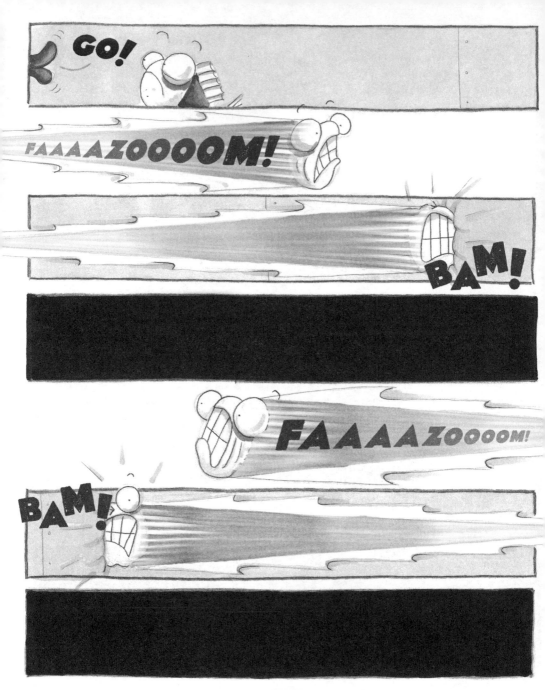

Listen, baby, I could do this ALL day.

But we're in a bit of a rush, and you have to stop crashing into walls, so we need to take this to the **NEXT LEVEL . . .**

Ready?

But I'll be a little fish-kebab!

You think I'd let that
happen to you?
I *believe* in you, sweet cheeks.
All you have to do is

TURN.

I KNOW you can do it.

GO!

· CHAPTER 6 ·
THE
BAD GIRLS

Yeah.
Well, I've seen better.

Nope.

Oh sure.
Anyone can lift a **FRIDGE,**
a **CHAINSAW,** and a
SECRET AGENT
off the ground using only their
MIND . . .

So . . . why don't we get Agent Fox to sing a little opera . . .

And let's start up that chainsaw . . .

GRRRRING!

GRRRRRING!!

YAWN

Oh, c'mon!
That was *awesome*!

Hey, Fox? Can you take over?
Mr. Remarkable's cheap tricks
are really bumming me out.

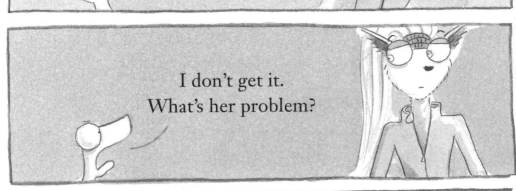

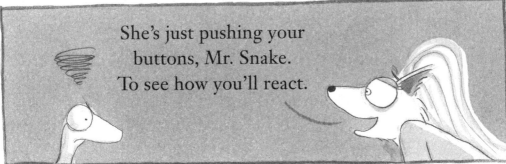

Yeah, I get it.

YOU SUPER-SHINY-HERO-LADIES

think we're NOTHING, don't you?

We're just a bunch of dirty crooks, right?

You don't think we've got what it takes.

None of you do.

But let me tell you something—

You don't know me AT ALL.

YOU KNOW

NOTHING

ABOUT ME.

Wow.

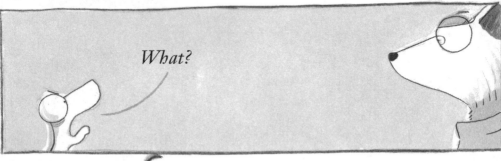

What?

You STILL don't get it, do you?

Get WHAT?!

Where I come from,
they **HUNT** foxes, Mr. Snake. For fun.
Because they think we're worthless
dirty thieves who don't deserve to live.

When I was young . . .

I lost everything.

Well, they told her early on that she couldn't be on the playground with the other kids because she had a **WILD SIDE.**

Eventually, that made her pretty angry, too.

And **AGENT HOGWILD**
was *told* her whole life she was bad.
So guess what?
She started *acting* like she was bad.

AGENT DOOM
was picked on every single day
for being a "creepy weirdo" . . .

And nobody even
wanted to go near
AGENT SHORTFUSE.
Ever.

But then, somehow, we found each other.

And we made a pact.

We decided to take all our hurt and our anger and our fear and turn it all into something **GOOD.**

Instead of trying to hurt those who'd hurt us, we started trying to

PROTECT THOSE WHO CAN'T PROTECT THEMSELVES.

So, don't you see, Mr. Snake?

We *are* you.

· CHAPTER 7 ·
THE FINAL EXAM

They'll stretch as much as you need, Major Big Butt.

Put them away for now though, Mr. Wolf. There's something you guys need to do first . . .

MOMENTS LATER . . .

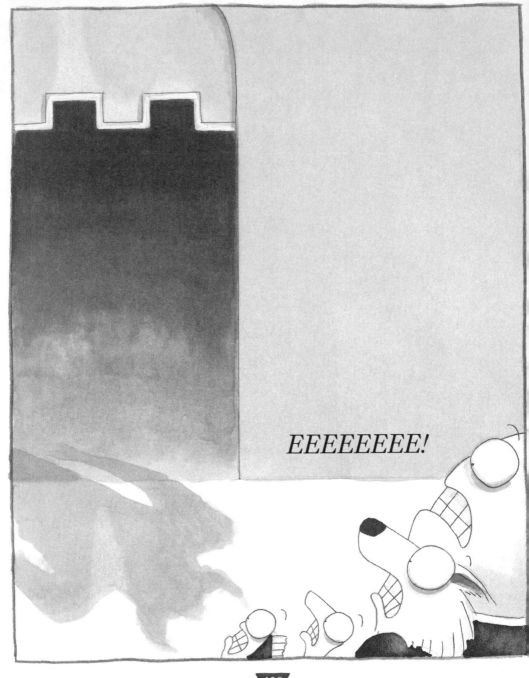

EEEEEEEE!

Huh?

This is your
FINAL TRAINING EXERCISE.
It's simple—*put Agent Shortfuse in the box.*
Good luck, gentlemen.

Oh man, I was worried there for a second. OK, Agent Shortfuse, we can do this the **EASY WAY** or—

Any suggestions?

I'm trying to **HOLD HER WITH MY MIND,** but she takes me out before I can focus.

She's too fast and too strong. None of us can take her **ALONE.**

WHISPER!
WHISPER!
WHISPER!
WHISPER!

Ready?

In your face,
Shortfuse!
You can't catch me!

And
while he
distracts
her . . .

ABOVE!

· CHAPTER 8 ·
A MARVELOUS PLAN

OPERATION TARANTULA

Ladies and gentlemen, I have developed a **PLAN** to give us the upper hand in this struggle against the Alien Forces. I call it—*Operation Tarantula*!

No offense, but you've named it after the only guy without superpowers?

Really?

WE don't have superpowers. You got a problem with THAT?!

It's elementary! Mr. Tarantula is the **ONLY** individual in the room capable of **OPERATING AN ALIEN SPACECRAFT,** is he not?

That's not true. I could *totally* do it.

And **OPERATION DOOM** would sound totes cooler.

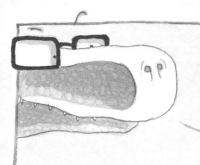

Hmmm. But are you small enough to sneak into the control deck of the mother ship **WITHOUT BEING NOTICED?**

NO! YOU ARE *NOT*! The **ONLY** way we can stop this invasion is to take charge of the mother ship and turn it against them. Therefore! The mission is to

SNEAK MR. TARANTULA ON BOARD,

any way we can.

But what about all the aliens **ON BOARD?** Who will protect Legs? He can't go in there alone . . .

Oh no, dear boy. He won't be alone . . .

Yeah . . . that could work.

Sounds good to me.

MY TEAM will take on the aliens here on the *ground*. We'll keep them off you as long as we can.

· CHAPTER 9 ·
BIG TROUBLE

SQUEEEEAALL!

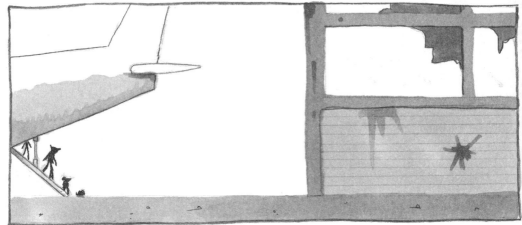

This is it,
Mr. Wolf.

Are you OK?

I . . .
I just feel a little . . .

You'll do *great*.

Man.
You two are
something else.

But you know what?

We wouldn't last
five minutes without you.

ZIZZZZZZZ!

MR. WOLF?!

HI, EVERYONE! IT'S MARMALADE!
MISS ME?!
I'D JUST LIKE TO SAY YOU REALLY ARE A GREAT EXAMPLE TO OTHERS, MR. WOLF.
YOU'VE REALLY TURNED YOUR LIFE AROUND, HAVEN'T YOU?
IT'S SO IMPRESSIVE!

AND IT ALMOST MAKES ME FEEL **BAD** ABOUT DOING **THIS**—

The Three Little Pigs were *right?!*

Mr. Wolf is **BADDER**—and **BIGGER**—than ever.
And he's coming to **DESTROY** your town in

the BAD GUYS

in The Big Bad Wolf!